Marie

Written by Kitty Richards
Illustrated by Sara Storino, Silvano Scolari,
and The Disney Storybook Artists

Disney
PRESS

New York

With love to the Biscuit

Printed in Singapore
First Edition
1 3 5 7 9 10 8 6 4 2
Library of Congress Catalog Card Number: 2005936780
ISBN: 1-4231-0058-1
Visit www.disneybooks.com

Bonjour! I am Marie. My family and I live in this fancy house in Paris. (That's in France, you know.) We are the treasured pets of Madame Adelaide Bonfamille. She calls us her children. Once, we were catnapped by Madame's old butler, Edgar. It was in all the papers. But that's another story. *This* story is all about me!

Why don't you turn the page and take a look inside our home. . . .

This is my brother Berlioz. Someday he will be a famous composer, just like his namesake.

My brother Toulouse loves to paint. Someday he will be famous, too. He's named after an important artist.

And here's a portrait that Toulouse painted. It's a picture of Edgar, the mean butler.

This is Abraham De Lacey Giuseppe Casey Thomas O'Malley. We used to call him Mr. O'Malley, but now we call him Papa.

And here is my mama, Duchess. She always reminds my brothers and me to be lovely and charming ladies and gentlemen.

Madame says that someday I will be as beautiful as my mama. It's true, I *do* have sparkling sapphire eyes that dazzle, just like hers!

Here's what I like:

Singing my arpeggios. One day
I will be a famous prima donna,
just like Madame was!

Wrestling with my
brothers—but only
when Mama's not
watching!

Going shopping
with Madame.

And most of all . . .
I like exploring Paris
with my friend,
Roquefort, Jr.

And today, we're going to do just that!

"Have fun, darlings, look both ways before you cross the street, and be home by seven o'clock tonight for a lovely surprise!" says Mama.

Ooh! That's another thing I like—lovely surprises!

"Au revoir, Marie!" Mama calls. "And don't forget to always be a lady!"

"I won't," I promise. "Forget to be a lady, I mean," I add, just in case there is any confusion.

Roquefort and I both love to walk
along the Seine, the river that divides
the city of Paris. There's so much to see!

"To Les Grand Magasins du Louvre?" asks Roquefort, Jr.
"To Les Grand Magasins du Louvre!" I reply.

That just happens to be my favorite, favorite, *favorite* department store. We head straight for the perfume counter.

Roquefort knows it is important for a lady to smell beautiful. And nobody seems to mind if we sample the perfume!

We both agree that our next stop should be La Cathédrale de Notre Dame de Paris, or Notre Dame for short. Paris has many wonderful buildings and churches, and Notre Dame is probably the most famous. That's because it's so beautiful. Visitors come from all over the world to admire the stained glass and architecture.

But here's what Roquefort likes best—making faces at the gargoyles!

And here's what I like best—chasing the pigeons!

A stroll through one of Paris's many parks is always the fashionable thing to do. One of our favorites is Le Jardin des Tuileries.

Roquefort likes to
take in a little theater...

...while I enjoy boating.

Oh, look—it's the Gabble sisters!
"See you tonight, Marie!" they call.

Roquefort, Jr. and I are hungry. He has his heart set on cheese.

"Can we stop here, s'il vous plaît?" he begs, pointing to a cheese shop.

I give him a boost so he can see in the window.

"Look at all that cheese, Marie!" he says wistfully.

Frankly, I prefer cream, but then again, I am not a mouse.

"Au revoir, Roquefort," I say. "Enjoy the cheese shop! I will pick you up on my way home."

I stroll over to my favorite café. I am a regular, and the waiter greets me: "Bonjour, Marie, one crème de la crème de Les Deux Magots?"

I nod and sit under my usual table.

There is nothing as wonderful as sitting at an outside table at your favorite café and watching the world go by.

This café is especially popular with artists and writers, so I feel right at home. One of the artists paints my portrait while I eat.

His name is Pablo . . . Pablo Picasso. Perhaps you've heard of him?

After lunch, I decide to pay a visit to the Eiffel Tower. The view of my city from the top is unparalleled.

When I get back down to the ground, I realize how late it has become. Oh dear, it is time to collect Roquefort and make our way home. But how will I get there in time? There must be a way!

Then I spot it—the perfect Paris transportation!

Oui, oui! Traveling by bicycle c'est magnifique!

I arrive at La Fromagerie just in time. Roquefort is about to become dinner!

I try to reason with the kitten.

Then I try again.

Then I try another tactic.

It works.

Here's the thing about ladies.
They never start fights,
but they certainly do
finish them!

It is time to head home.

"Darlings! You are home,"
says Mama. "And you are
just in time for . . .

. . . Scat Cat and the swingin' hepcats!"

J'adore Paris, don't you?